PRETTY TO BE
DARK-SKINNED

By
Mijiza A. Green

ALPHA BOOK PUBLISHING

4132 E. JOPPA RD. #1123

NOTTINGHAM, MD 21236

Contact (888)-257-4229

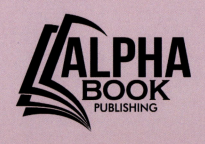

This Book belongs to...

Mimi loves to play outside and jump rope. She loves chocolate cake, chocolate ice cream, and chocolate candy.
She loved it so much that her mom even called her Chocolate.
She would pull her arms and dance with her and say, "That's my pretty chocolate girl."

Mimi loved it when she said that. It made her feel beautiful, like the prettiest girl in the world.

But something still was missing. Mimi always felt different from everyone else. She had a different complexion from the rest of her family.
But her family always told her she was pretty to be dark-skinned.

Mimi's skin was so dark, that her siblings would sing a song while she got washed up in the family room:
"I see your hiney... all black and shiny..." is the song that made her cry each time, as they sang and danced around her. But afterwards, they would say, "Oh, shush, we are just playing—you are pretty to be dark-skinned."

Mimi's skin was so dark, that her friends at school would call her Blackey, African Boombada, Tar Baby, even Midnight. But teachers would say to her, "Don't worry about what the kids say, you are very pretty to be dark-skinned."

Mimi's skin color was so different, her mom's friends would joke and say she was the milkman's baby—insisting that she did not belong to her family.
Her mom's friends would say, "But she is so pretty to be dark-skinned."

Though Mimi was dark, she knew in her heart she was special. She knew there had to be something good about her, but she just didn't know what it was.

Mimi's real name was Mijiza...a name that no one could pronounce properly. When people tried, they would say, "That's a pretty name for a pretty, dark-skinned girl."

Mimi had eczema on her skin so kids stayed away from her and called her ugly.
Doctors would say, "She is pretty to be dark. Her skin will get better. Just use this special oatmeal soap."

Mimi stuttered every time she spoke, and was often told by her family to shut up, or she would just cry and stop speaking because she couldn't get a word out.
People said, if she just didn't talk all the time, it wouldn't bring so much attention to her stuttering— that she was lucky she was pretty to be a dark-skinned girl.

Mimi was heavier than the kids in her classes, so she had to wear grown-up-sized clothes when she was just a little girl. Kids made fun of her because she was bigger; the boys called her names like Big Butt, Big Booty Judy, or Thickums.
The counselors at school would say, "You will thin out in time. You're pretty to be a dark girl, just show them how smart you are."
So, she was the second smartest in her school and continued to achieve the honor roll, but it didn't change what people saw from the outside.
All she was or would ever be was the pretty dark-skinned girl.

Mimi was jealous of all the light-skinned girls in her class, and she was starting to dislike her family as well because they all had complexions that were lighter than hers.

Everywhere she went, she was treated differently: in school, at home—there was just no safe place for her. Everything about Mimi was different. It often left her crying and sad each day.

Mimi found new ways of hiding her sadness. She tried to wear bright colors. That didn't work. She wore oversized clothes to hide her shape. That didn't work. She joked a lot about other people and often made jokes about herself before anyone else could. But she still didn't feel happy.

Life got even worse for her; she began getting in trouble in class, talking back to teachers, and often found herself picking a fight with anyone who said the wrong thing.
Nothing seemed to change what she was feeling on the inside, and nothing she did seemed to ever change the way people saw her from the outside. She would always be the dark-skinned girl. No one seemed to care about the other things she had to offer, like being smart, funny, or creative.

Her parents got a phone call home one day from the principal, who had behavior concerns. Mimi had never been in serious trouble. She was afraid to go home. When she arrived at home, she was greeted by her mom and dad.

She put her head down when they asked her what was going on and why was her behavior changing.

She began to cry and tell them all the things people said to her. They hugged her so tight...she never felt so happy. For the first time she felt loved, she felt like she belonged, she felt like she mattered.

She looked at them and said, "Why do I look so different? Why did you name me Mijiza? Why does everyone treat me different? Why do I have eczema? Why do I stutter? Why did you make me so dark?"

They said, "Because you are different; you are unique. You are wonderfully made in God's eyes. From the moment we saw you, we knew you were destined for great things."

They said, "Mijiza, your name means, works well with her hands; it was a special name for our special girl. A girl with this name will have a great deal of self-confidence and will achieve success. She will work hard. She will have a high standard of honesty. She will be dependable. She will be serious-minded and practical about everything she does. We knew who you were when we saw you. Your hands will create and deliver great gifts to others. With your beautiful, dark-skinned hands, you will change the world and how they see dark-skinned girls."

She smiled as she asked her dad, "Am I pretty to be dark-skinned?"

He said, "Baby girl, you are not pretty to be dark-skinned; you are just pretty—Period." He said, "Don't let people add words behind that statement. You have to believe that you are pretty, that you do belong, and that you are loved by all, especially your family, and that's what matters most."

Things finally started to change. It was not the people who had changed, it was her. Mijiza loved her name even more, she no longer went by Mimi. Her confidence and self-esteem began to grow. Now when she looked in the mirror she would sing, "I am pretty. I am pretty." She learned more about her name, she studied more about her heritage. She loved her dark skin.

Mijiza loved herself more and more, and all that came with it, her stuttering, her eczema, and her dark complexion. As she grew older, she learned how to take her time when speaking which helped her to stop stuttering. She learned to speak well when in front of audiences.
Her eczema cleared up and she created natural skin products to keep it that way.

When Mijiza grew up, she started a mentor group to help girls who were facing the same issues, to help build their self-esteem and self-love.
She now knew what she felt was real. She was different. She was made to change the world one girl at a time.

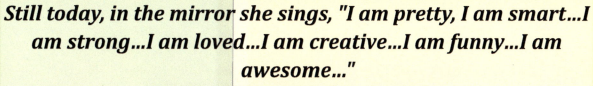

Still today, in the mirror she sings, "I am pretty, I am smart...I am strong...I am loved...I am creative...I am funny...I am awesome..."
The list goes on and on and on...
The End.

THE END

About The Author

Mijiza Green was born in Brooklyn, NY. She moved to Maryland in 2001. Mrs. Green is a 2021 graduate of Morgan State University, majoring in psychology. She has worked with children for over 15 years for Harford County Public Schools and several other organizations. She is the creator of Treasured Jewels Mentor Program, designed to impact, inspire and educate young girls ages 7-17. She also founded Grace Empowerment & Young Men Empowered, designed for troubled youth facing criminal records. Mrs. Green is an advocate for change in her community. Some say she is the glue that holds the community, and schools together. She is a voice for every child she encounters and has a motto: "Going from being distracted to directed." She believes that there is always room for improvement and that every child needs to be loved and listened to in order to develop relationships that lead to change.

Mijiza is married to Nathanal Green Jr. She is the mother of three boys: Vincent, Caleb and Noah, one stepdaughter: Niyah Green, and Nana to 2 beautiful grandchildren:

Laylah and Vincent Jr.

Made in the USA
Middletown, DE
15 January 2021